D0177187

The Black Cat

ALLAN AHLBERG • ANDRÉ AMSTUTZ

PUFFIN

In a dark dark town,
on a cold cold night,
under a starry starry sky,
down a slippery slippery slope,
on a bumpety bumpety sledge . . .

a little skeleton is sliding . . .
and sliding . . .
and crashing – wallop!

The little skeleton
loses a leg in the snow.
A white leg in snow
is hard to find.
A black cat in snow
is *easy* to find.
What is *she* doing here?

The little skeleton and the big skeleton
go to the bone-yard
to get a new leg
for the little skeleton.

They play around with the bones
for a while . . .
and go home to bed.

Then . . .
in the dark dark town,
on *another* cold cold night,
under a starry starry sky,
down a slippery slippery slope,
on a bumpety bumpety sledge . . .

two skeletons are sliding . . .
and sliding . . .
and sliding . . .
and crashing – bang!
WALLOP!
This time the big skeleton
loses a leg in the snow.

CRASH

A white leg in snow
is hard to find.
A black cat is easy.
Is she still here?
I wonder why.

three skeletons are sliding . . .
and sliding . . .
and shouting . . .
and barking!
And banging! Wallop!

CRASH!!

This time the big skeleton
and the little skeleton
lose the dog skeleton.
A white dog in snow
is hard to find.
But a noisy dog is easy to find.
So is a black cat!

Woof!

The dog skeleton chases the cat.
Now we know –
that's what she is here for!

The dog chases the cat
up and down
the dark dark hill,
in and out
of the dark dark bone-yard,

round and round
the dark dark streets
and down and down
to the dark dark cellar.

But a black cat in a cellar
is very hard to find.
Can *you* see her?

Well, the dog skeleton couldn't,
and the little skeleton couldn't,
and the big skeleton didn't even try.
So off they went – at last – to bed.

Meanwhile . . .
in the same town,
on the same night,
under the same sky,
down the same slope,
a bumpety sledge is sliding . . .

with a black cat on it.

PUFFIN BOOKS

Published by the Penguin Group
Penguin Books Ltd, 80 Strand, London WC2R 0RL, England
Penguin Group (USA), Inc., 375 Hudson Street, New York, New York 10014, USA
Penguin Books Australia Ltd, 250 Camberwell Road, Camberwell, Victoria 3124, Australia
Penguin Books Canada Ltd, 10 Alcorn Avenue, Toronto, Ontario, Canada M4V 3B2
Penguin Books India (P) Ltd, 11 Community Centre, Panchsheel Park, New Delhi 110 017, India
Penguin Group (NZ), cnr Airborne and Rosedale Roads, Albany, Auckland 1310, New Zealand
Penguin Books (South Africa) (Pty) Ltd, 24 Sturdee Avenue, Rosebank 2196, South Africa

Penguin Books Ltd, Registered Offices: 80 Strand, London WC2R 0RL, England

www.penguin.com

First published by William Heinemann Ltd 1990
First published in Puffin Books 2004
3 5 7 9 10 8 6 4

Text copyright © Allan Ahlberg, 1990
Illustrations copyright © André Amstutz, 1990
All rights reserved

The moral right of the author and illustrator has been asserted

Set in Bembo

Manufactured in China

British Library Cataloguing in Publication Data
A CIP catalogue record for this book is available from the British Library

ISBN-13: 978-0-14056-680-2
ISBN-10: 0-14056-680-5